MY VERY OWN BOOK

COSTUMES

Designed by

Early costume

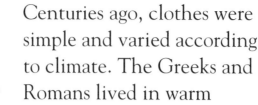 Centuries ago, clothes were simple and varied according to climate. The Greeks and Romans lived in warm climates and so wore simple clothes. The Vikings lived in colder climates, and so wore warmer clothes. Later on, clothes became more elaborate and fashion played an important part in daily life.

Roman governor
The purple banding on this toga shows its wearer to be an important person in Roman society.

Gladiator's helmet
The bronze helmet worn by Roman gladiators was very strong. But the brim was so big that it was hard to see out. The crest on the top was just for show.

Man and woman from ancient Greece
In ancient Greece, men and women dressed alike. They wore a straight tunic, called a chiton. It was made from a single rectangle of cloth, cut into two and fastened from the neck to the elbows to make it more graceful.

Greek warrior
Ancient Greek soldiers wore a solid helmet and breastplate when they went into battle. Their short tunic allowed them to run freely.

A hardy Viking
Vikings lived in cold climates and so needed warm clothes. They wore woolen pants, tunics, and fur wraps to keep out the wind and rain.

Roman legionary
Roman legionaries were well-armed and protected. They carried a javelin, a dagger, and a sword.

Italian courtiers
In the 15th century, the Italians wore the best clothes they could afford. Both men's and women's clothes were often made from richly decorated silks, and were sometimes interwoven with real gold or silver thread.

Courtly woman
Some of the headdresses worn in 14th-century Europe were very elaborate.

Lady of the manor
This lady is wearing a long, slim, flowing dress. Her hair is hidden by a veil.

Armed knight
In the 15th century, knights wore plates of armor. Each piece was strapped on to the body.

A nobleman's son
In the 14th century, young pages dressed like adult knights. They wore thick tunics with puffed sleeves and thick tights.

Lord of the manor
The rich lords of Burgundy in France wore clothes like this in the 15th century. This lord wears black leather boots and carries a belt, and a dagger on his purse.

Early platforms
Some women wore chopines over their shoes in wet weather. These platforms could be 30 in (75 cm) high.

1500 to 1800

The wealth of Europe during this period is reflected in the rich clothes that were worn. In Germany, people wore brightly colored clothes decorated with slashing, that is cut fabric that allows the material underneath to show through. The Spanish favored capes and large ruffs. In the 17th century, the flamboyance of the French court influenced fashions. It was Louis XIV who introduced the periwig, later known as the wig.

Golden armor
This suit of armor is decorated with gold. The breastplate has followed the fashion of the day by becoming more pointed at the waist. The bulging hips allow for thick underwear to be worn underneath.

Spanish courtier
This fashionable courtier is wearing ruffs at the neck and wrist. His doublet is thickly padded to form a V-shape at the waist.

16th-century hand-stitched shoe
In England, shoes became so wide that Henry VIII ordered people to wear shoes no wider than 6 in (15 cm) across.

16th-century boy
English boys from noble families dressed like their king, Henry VIII. They wore embroidered tunics, coats, and velvet hats.

Flexible foot armor
Soldiers in the 16th century wore foot armor that could bend in the middle. The strong metal plates were joined together with hinges.

CHILDREN

Street-wise kid

Aristocrat's daughter

Working-class schoolchild

A tradesman's son

A nobleman's son

Victorian girl with ringlets

16th-century boy

Girl in a bustle dress

A young hippy in beads

Greek boy in a short tunic

HATS

Roman
gladiator's
helmet

1920's silver silk hat

Army
officer's
shako

Sailor's straw hat

Cloche hat
from the 1920s

First World
War red straw hat

Coachman's top hat

Dr Stanley's
bush hat

Baby's
bonnet
with hoops

Mexican
sombrero with a
sugarloaf crown

MEN

Face patches

Lord of the manor

Professional gentleman

Stylish Italian courtier

1920's country gentleman

American cowboy

Ancient Greek man

Roman governor

Fashionable French gentleman

Spanish courtier

Serious Victorian gentleman

WOMEN

Bathing beauty

Graceful Grecian woman

Lady in silk bustle dress

1930's society lady

Italian woman in brocade

Courtly woman

Floral sunsuit

The New Look

Victorian woman dressing in a crinoline cage

Victorian woman wearing a crinoline

Lady of the manor

SHOES AND BOOTS

1960's knee-length boots

Military bucket-top boots

Cycling boots, worn with bloomers

A brocade shoe clog

Flexible foot armor

Leather mules

A 17th-century silk shoe

Button-up ladies' boots

Cowboy boots

Hand-stitched leather shoe

Men's platform shoes

Early platform shoes

WARRIORS

Knight in golden armor

German knight in armor

French fusilier

Armed knight in armor plating and chain mail

American soldier in combat uniform

A hardy Viking

Japanese samurai

Greek warrior

Roman legionary

Airman in the British Air Force

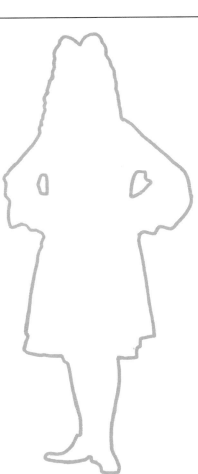

Professional gentleman
Long vests, loose breeches, and velvet coats were very fashionable in the 18th century.

Face patches
By the end of the 18th century, men wore long, narrow coats, floral vests, and powdered wigs on their heads. On their faces they wore beauty patches in the shape of suns, moons, or stars.

German knight in armor
In the early 16th century, pleats were very fashionable. The ridges in this suit of armor imitate the pleated clothing of the time.

French gentleman
Men's suits came into fashion in the 17th century. Jackets were long and pants were short.

Silk shoes
In the 17th century, shoes had high heels and bows. This pair is made of silk.

Brocade shoe clog
Some 18th-century women wore a special clog in wet weather to keep their shoes dry.

Military bucket-top boots
Bucket-top boots could be worn folded up for riding, or down for walking.

Buttoned boot
This slim boot enabled women to show off their shapely ankles.

5

The 19th century

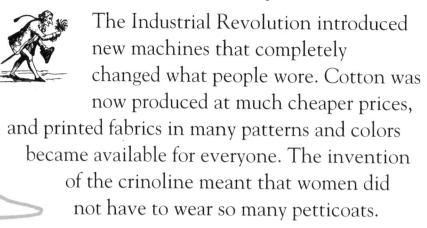

The Industrial Revolution introduced new machines that completely changed what people wore. Cotton was now produced at much cheaper prices, and printed fabrics in many patterns and colors became available for everyone. The invention of the crinoline meant that women did not have to wear so many petticoats.

Silk bustle dress
Women wore S-shaped silk dresses, called bustles. The bustle was made by a cushion or a frame worn under the skirt.

Victorian gentleman
By 1850 almost all men wore black, navy, or gray frock coats with check, plaid, or striped pants and vests.

Victorian girl
Girls wore plenty of pretty petticoats as well as pantaloons (long underwear) under their dressses.

Girl in bustle dress
This girl is wearing an original red wool bustle dress from 1880.

Working-class schoolchild
Children from poor families wore simple, more practical clothes with little decoration

For indoors only
When fashionable ladies were entertaining guests at home, they wore fancy leather slippers called mules.

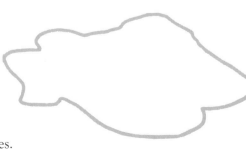

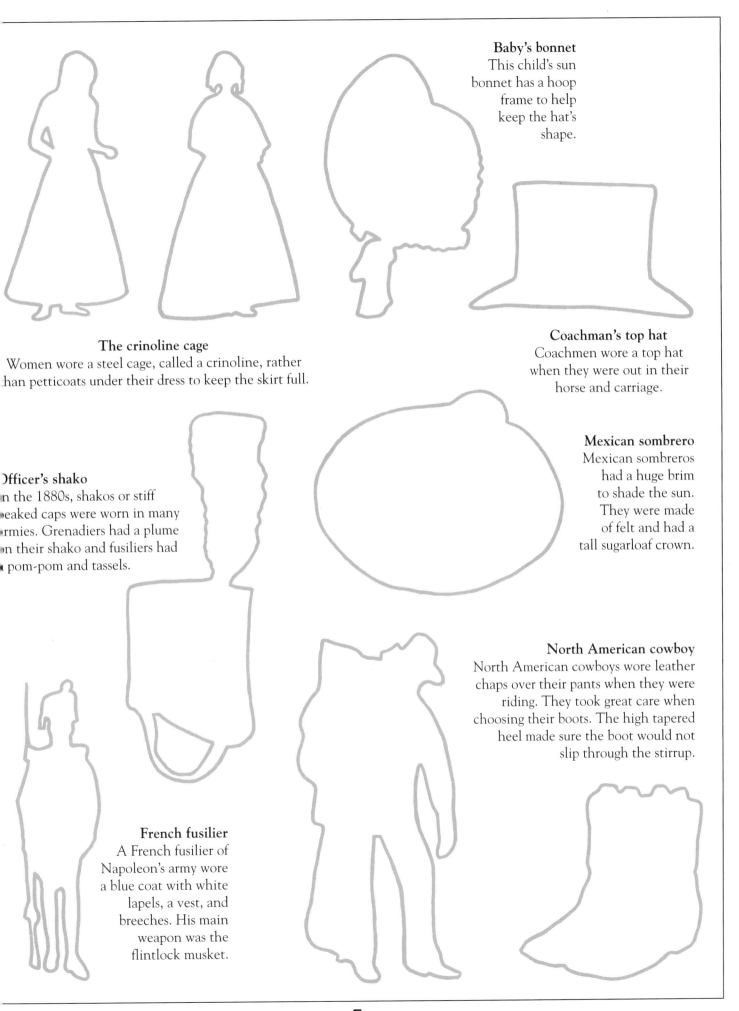

Baby's bonnet
This child's sun bonnet has a hoop frame to help keep the hat's shape.

Coachman's top hat
Coachmen wore a top hat when they were out in their horse and carriage.

The crinoline cage
Women wore a steel cage, called a crinoline, rather than petticoats under their dress to keep the skirt full.

Mexican sombrero
Mexican sombreros had a huge brim to shade the sun. They were made of felt and had a tall sugarloaf crown.

Officer's shako
In the 1880s, shakos or stiff peaked caps were worn in many armies. Grenadiers had a plume on their shako and fusiliers had a pom-pom and tassels.

North American cowboy
North American cowboys wore leather chaps over their pants when they were riding. They took great care when choosing their boots. The high tapered heel made sure the boot would not slip through the stirrup.

French fusilier
A French fusilier of Napoleon's army wore a blue coat with white lapels, a vest, and breeches. His main weapon was the flintlock musket.

7

The 20th century

Sports, dancing, motor cars, and American films all left their mark on fashion in the early years of this century. During World War II, clothes were made to last because materials were in short supply. After the war, Christian Dior launched the New Look for women, who now wore long, full skirts. New, daring styles were adopted in the 1960s, and by the early 1970s fashions changed again with the "hippy" look.

Red straw hat
At the beginning of the 20th century, respectable men and women were never seen out without some sort of hat.

1930's society lady
Women wore soft, flowing dresses during the 1930s.

The New Look
Dior's New Look was so glamorous that it was often copied by other designers.

Country gent
Gentlemen had a special sporting outfit for the country. They wore knee-length pants called "plus fours," a bow tie, and a tweed cap.

1960's boots
Long, zip-up boots were popular in the 1960s.

Floral sunsuit
Sunsuits were popular in the 1940s. This one has short puffed sleeves and a floral design.

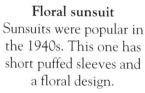

Streetwise kid
Jeans, T-shirts, and sneakers are worn today by young people all over the world.

Men's platform shoes
In the 1970s, platform shoes were often brightly colored.

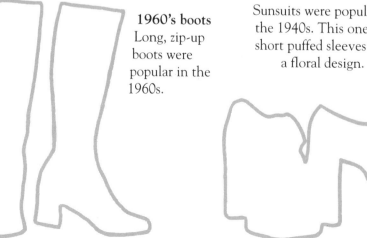